LUCY DANIELS

Little Animal Ark™

The Brave Bunny

Hodder
Children's
Books

A division of Hachette Children's Books

To Tabitha and Hannah

Special thanks to Linda Chapman

Little Animal Ark is a trademark of Working Partners Limited
Text copyright © 2001 Working Partners Limited
Created by Working Partners Limited, London, W6 0QT
Illustrations copyright © 2001 Andy Ellis

First published in Great Britain in 2001 by Hodder Children's Books

This edition published in 2007

The rights of Lucy Daniels and Andy Ellis to be identified as the author
and illustrator of this work respectively have been asserted by them in
accordance with the Copyright, Designs and Patents Act 1988.

1

A Catalogue record for this book is available from the
British Library

ISBN-13: 978 0 340 93253 7

Printed and bound in Great Britain by Clays Ltd, St Ives plc

Hodder Children's Books
A division of Hachette Children's Books
338 Euston Road, London NW1 3BH

Chapter One

"Don't forget to take your reading books home with you, Class 3!" called Miss Rushton, Mandy Hope's teacher. "I'll see you all on Monday."

Mandy grabbed her bag and pulled on her coat. "Have a nice weekend, Miss!" she called, as she followed her friends out into the playground.

"Mandy! Over here!"

Mandy's grandad was
standing next to Mr Baker, whose
daughter, Laura, was in Class 1.
Mandy ran over to them.

"Hello, Grandad," she said. "How come you're here to collect me?"

"Your mum's had to go up to Giant's Farm," her grandad explained. "One of Mr Grove's cows has been taken ill. And your dad's at the animal sanctuary."

Mandy nodded. Her mum and dad were both vets. They often had to leave their surgery, Animal Ark, to visit sick animals.

Just then, Laura Baker came charging across the playground, her dark curly hair bouncing about. "Hi, Dad!" she cried, flinging herself into Mr Baker's arms. She swung round. "Hi, Mandy!"

Mr Baker smiled. "Mandy's grandad's just been giving me some advice on growing vegetables, Laura. He's offered to come and take a look at my lettuces."

"What? Now?" Laura asked. When her father nodded, she

looked very excited. "You can come and see Nibbles, my new rabbit, Mandy!" she said.

"What colour is he?" Mandy asked. She loved rabbits.

"Black and white," Laura told her, her eyes shining. "He's really cute. But he's only four months old, and a bit shy."

Mr Baker shook his head. "Laura's rabbit mad," he said. "I hope you don't mind talking about rabbits all the way home, Mandy!"

Mandy grinned. She couldn't think of anything nicer. "Oh, no, I *love* talking about animals!" she said.

Chapter Two

When they reached the Bakers'
house, Mr Baker took them
through the wooden side gate,
into the back garden. Mr Baker
and Grandad headed towards the
vegetable patch.

Laura took Mandy's hand
and pulled her towards the
bottom of the garden. "Come and
see Nibbles!" she said. She led
Mandy to a large wooden hutch.

Mandy crouched down. Behind the wire mesh was a young black and white rabbit.

He sat back and looked at Mandy with bright, dark eyes. His whiskers wobbled nervously. Then slowly, he hopped over and stood up on his hind legs to say hello.

"He's sweet!" Mandy said softly. She reached out a finger and gently tickled Nibbles through the wire.

Laura nodded happily. "He seems to like you," she said. "You can hold him, if you like." She opened the hutch and lifted Nibbles out.

Mandy took the young rabbit from Laura's arms. She was careful to support his back legs just like her mum and dad had shown her.

Nibbles cuddled in close. "Oh, he's really gorgeous!" Mandy said, feeling his soft fur and the quick patter of his heartbeat.

"Why did you call him Nibbles?"

"Because he nibbles
everything!" Laura said with a
laugh. "His food, treats, bedding –
he even nibbles at his cage and
water bottle."

Just then, the back door of the cottage opened and a small boy came running out into the garden. "Laura!" he shouted. "Auntie Katie said you were home from school!"

"Tom!" Laura said in surprise, as the little boy ran towards them. "What are you doing here?"

"Mummy and I came round for tea," Tom said.

Laura turned to Mandy. "Tom's my cousin," she explained. "He's three."

Mandy smiled at the little boy. He had a round face and dark curls just like Laura. "Hi, Tom. I'm Mandy," she said.

But Tom wasn't listening. He was staring at Nibbles. "Can I hold your bunny, Laura? Can I? Please? Can I hold him?" he asked eagerly. "Can I? Please?"

"No, Tom," Laura said quickly.

"You're too little. You'll drop him."

"I won't, I promise!" Tom said loudly.

Nibbles squirmed in Mandy's arms. "Tom, you're frightening Nibbles," she said, gently. "He's only a baby – he doesn't like loud noises."

"*Sorry!*" Tom whispered.

"Maybe you should just stroke him, Tom," Laura said.

"But I want to *hold* him." Tom looked like he was about to cry.

"Well . . ." said Laura, frowning a little doubtfully. "Maybe you could just hold him for a *few* seconds."

"Oh, yes, please!" Tom whispered.

Laura took Nibbles from Mandy. "You must be really careful," she said as she handed him to Tom. "You mustn't let him go."

The little boy took the rabbit into his arms. For a moment, he stood there, beaming, but then Nibbles began to wriggle.

"Ooh! That tickles!" he laughed, forgetting to be quiet.

Frightened, Nibbles wriggled more. Tom tried to hang onto the struggling bunny. But he just couldn't keep hold. With one last kick, Nibbles twisted himself out of Tom's grasp and leaped to the ground!

Chapter Three

"Nibbles!" Laura cried in alarm.

Mandy moved quickly. She
threw herself onto the grass
and grabbed Nibbles.

The frightened bunny
struggled, his sharp claws
catching on Mandy's bare arms.

Mandy sat up and pulled him
close to her chest. She knew
Nibbles didn't mean to hurt her.
"It's OK, Nibbles," she soothed.

"Oh, Mandy!" Laura cried, dropping onto the grass beside her. "Is he all right?"

"He's fine," Mandy said, as she felt Nibbles settle in her arms.

"I didn't mean to drop him, Laura!" Tom gulped, tears welling in his eyes.

Mandy saw Laura frown and

spoke quickly. "We know you didn't mean it, Tom," she said. "You were just so excited."

Tom nodded.

"Would you like to stroke Nibbles while I hold him?" Mandy asked him.

"Yes, please," Tom whispered. Crouching down beside Mandy, he patted Nibbles very carefully. "I'm sorry, Laura," he said, looking up at his cousin.

Laura seemed to forgive him. She sighed. "That's all right. I should have known you were too little to hold him."

She took her rabbit from Mandy and put him in his run.

Nibbles shook himself for a moment and then hopped off quite happily across the grass.

"I wish I had a bunny," Tom said, as Nibbles turned and looked at them, his black nose twitching. Just then, they heard the sound of the back door opening.

Mrs Baker, Laura's mum, came out. "Tea-time!" she called.

Mandy followed Laura and Tom inside. Her grandad and Mr Baker were in the kitchen with Mrs Baker and Tom's mum.

"Mrs Baker's invited us to stay for tea," Grandad said to Mandy.

"Can we take ours upstairs, Mum?" Laura asked. "I want to show Mandy my bedroom."

"All right," Mrs Baker agreed.

Tom turned to his mum. "Can I take mine outside?" he asked.

His mum nodded. "Yes, but don't feed your sandwich to Nibbles," she warned him.

Tom's eyes widened. "I wouldn't, Mummy!"

Mandy and Laura went upstairs with their sandwiches and cake.

"My room's just been decorated," Laura said to Mandy. "Look!" She pushed open her bedroom door.

Mandy gasped. The room was covered with rabbits! There were rabbits on the wallpaper, rabbits on the curtains, rabbits on Laura's duvet – even the light-shade had a rabbit on it! "Wow!" she exclaimed. "You must *really* like rabbits, Laura. I've never seen so many!"

"Isn't it brilliant?" Laura said happily. She put her plate down and picked up a photo frame from her bedside table. "Look, this is Nibbles the day we got him."

Mandy looked at the picture of Nibbles. He looked cuter than ever, snuggled deep in Laura's arms, his bright eyes sparkling at the camera.

"I can see his hutch from my window," Laura said. She went to the window and looked out. "What's Tom doing?" she said with a sudden frown.

Mandy joined her. Tom wasn't eating his tea. He was running around the garden below, laughing happily. He seemed to be chasing something.

At exactly the same moment, Mandy and Laura gasped. Hopping along in front of Tom was Nibbles!

Chapter Four

Mandy and Laura raced downstairs. The grown-ups had moved through to the living room. Not stopping to get them, the two girls ran outside.

"Oh, Mandy! Nibbles will escape!" Laura panted.

Nibbles was hopping around near the fence at the bottom of the garden. He looked like he was having a wonderful time.

Every few hops, he would pause and nibble at a piece of grass or a nearby bush.

Tom ran along behind him, laughing.

"Tom!" Laura shouted, racing down the garden.

The little boy swung round. The smile left his face as he saw his angry cousin.

"What are you doing?"
Laura cried.

Seeing Nibbles begin to hop straight towards a gap in the fence, Mandy speeded up. She raced over, reaching the fence just before Nibbles did. The black and white rabbit stopped and looked at her.

"Come here, Nibbles," Mandy said, crouching down. But with a nervous flick of his ears, Nibbles turned and hopped away across the lawn.

"Don't chase him!" Mandy said, seeing Laura and Tom about to run after him. "He might panic even more!" Laura and Tom stopped and looked at her. "Let's try and close in on him quietly," Mandy told them.

Seeing that they had stopped, Nibbles paused too, and began to nibble at a patch of buttercups.

He kept a wary eye on them, his ears flickering as they began to creep towards him.

"Come here, Nibbles," Laura said softly. But as they got close, Nibbles bounded away again. "We'll never catch him!" she cried.

"Are there any treats that he really likes?" Mandy asked. "Some carrot or cabbage or something? Maybe then we could get him to come to us."

"He loves dried apple pieces," Laura said. "I'll go and fetch some!"

Leaving Mandy and Tom to make sure that Nibbles didn't escape from the garden, she ran into the house.

She returned a few minutes later with a bag of dried apple. "Here," she said, pushing the bag into Mandy's hand.

"OK," said Mandy, her eyes glued on the little rabbit. "Let's creep up very slowly. When we get near, I'll try and get close to him using these."

They began to move in on Nibbles. He looked round at them.

"Here we are, Nibbles," Mandy called softly. She crouched down and held out a piece of apple. "Look what I've got!"

At first, she thought the bunny was going to run away again. But suddenly, his nose twitched as he caught the scent of his favourite treat. Slowly, he hopped towards Mandy.

Mandy waited until he was very close to her and then dropped the piece of apple on the ground.

As Nibbles bent down to snatch it in his teeth, Mandy flung herself down and grabbed him. "Got you!" she said softly.

Laura and Tom ran over.

"Oh, Nibbles!" Laura said. "It's naughty to run away like that! "

A yellow buttercup petal quivered on Nibbles's nose. He didn't look very naughty.  In fact, he looked quite relieved to be safe in Mandy's arms!

Mandy grinned and wiped the petal away. "I think it's time you went back in your hutch," she said to the little rabbit. "That's enough adventures for one day!"

*

Back at Animal Ark that evening, Mandy told her mum and dad all about Nibbles and his trip around Laura's garden.

"Well, at least it all ended happily!" Mrs Hope said with a laugh.

"For Nibbles, anyway," said Mandy. "Laura's cousin got told off!"

Just then, the phone rang.

"I'll get it," Mr Hope said. He got up from his armchair, and went into the hall.

Mandy watched her dad through the doorway as he picked up the receiver.

"Animal Ark – Adam Hope speaking," he said.

There was a pause, then Mandy saw a serious look cross her dad's face. "Of course, Mr Baker," he said quickly. "Bring him here now and I'll take a look at him."

"Mr Baker?" Mandy said, as her dad put the phone down. "Was that Laura's dad?"

Mr Hope nodded, his face grave. "Laura and her father are bringing Nibbles to Animal Ark straight away, Mandy. He sounds very ill."

Chapter Five

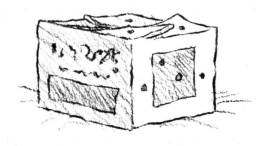

Although it was nearly Mandy's bedtime, her mum said that she could stay up and wait for Mr Baker to arrive.

Fifteen minutes later, there was a knock on the front door.

Mr Hope let Mr Baker and Laura in. Mr Baker was holding a cardboard box. "I'm sorry about calling round so late," he said.

Laura clung to her dad's side.

Her face was pale and she looked as if she had been crying.

"Bring Nibbles through to the examination room," Mr Hope said gently. "Let's have a look at him."

"Can I come too, Dad?" Mandy asked.

Her dad nodded, and she followed Laura and Mr Baker into the surgery.

Mr Baker put the box down on the examination table and took Nibbles out. The poor little rabbit sat in a huddled heap. His ears were flat and his eyes half-closed. He was trembling, too.

Mandy swallowed. Nibbles looked really ill!

Adam Hope stroked the rabbit. "So when did you notice that something was the matter?" he asked.

"Just over an hour ago," Mr Baker replied. "Laura went out to check on him."

"He was sitting all hunched up in a corner of his hutch," Laura said. "He didn't want to play or eat anything."

She looked at Nibbles, her eyes filling with tears. "I told Dad and he said that we should leave him for a bit to see if he got better. But he didn't get better, and now he's got an upset tummy."

Laura's dad gave her a hug. "It sounds as though he might have eaten something that disagreed with him," Mr Hope said thoughtfully. "Can you think of anything in the garden that might be poisonous – poppies, foxgloves, buttercups . . ."

"Buttercups!" Mandy gasped before Mr Baker or Laura could say a word. She remembered the yellow petal on Nibbles's nose. "He did eat some buttercups, Dad!"

Laura nodded. "Yes, I remember!"

"I didn't realise buttercups were poisonous," said Mr Baker, surprised.

"They're very poisonous to rabbits," Mr Hope said seriously. "If Nibbles has eaten some then he's going to be feeling very poorly." He turned to Laura. "I think Nibbles will have to stay here for a while, Laura."

Laura's lower lip wobbled and she clutched her dad's hand.

44

"But first, I'll give him a little injection to help stop his tummy hurting," said Mr Hope kindly. "Then we'll go and settle him down in one of the cages. He's too ill to drink, so I'll put him on a drip."

"Will that hurt him?" Laura whispered.

"Not at all," Mr Hope said. He gave Nibbles a quick injection, then picked him up. "Now, shall we go and make him comfy for the night?"

Laura nodded. They all went through to the residential unit. Animals who were too sick to go home stayed there.

Mr Hope settled Nibbles in one of the rabbit cages. He put a heat-pad under him to keep him warm. Then he fixed a drip to one of Nibbles's ears.

"I think we should leave him alone now," he said. "Nibbles will need all his strength to get well. Let's see how he is in the morning."

Chapter Six

Mandy found it hard to sleep that night. All she could think about was Nibbles. What if he didn't get better?

As soon as she heard her parents start to get up, she jumped out of bed and ran into their room.

"Mandy!" her mum said, looking round in surprise. "Whatever is wrong?"

"Can we go and see how Nibbles is?" Mandy asked, looking at her dad.

"It's very early," Mr Hope said.

"Please!" Mandy pleaded.

Mr Hope looked at Mandy's worried face and nodded. "All right," he said. Pulling on his dressing gown, he followed Mandy downstairs.

Nibbles was lying in his cage. He wasn't hunched up, like he had been the night before, but he didn't look very well. He was still trembling a little.

Mr Hope opened the cage door and checked Nibbles over.

"Oh, Dad," Mandy said. "He is going to get better, isn't he?"

"I did warn you that he's really not very well, Mandy," Mr Hope said quietly. He ran his hands over the rabbit's coat.

"I've given him all the medicine I can. Now, it's up to him. He has to fight to get better." He closed the door of the cage.

"Can I stay with him, Dad?" Mandy asked.

"Not just now, love," Mr Hope said. "Let him rest a bit more. Come back and see him after breakfast."

*

When Mandy returned, Nibbles was still lying quietly on his blanket. She stared at him through the wire front of the cage. "Oh, Nibbles, you've *got* to be brave!" she whispered. She opened the cage door and stroked him gently.

The little rabbit opened
his eyes. For a moment his nose
twitched. Mandy had the feeling
that being stroked comforted him,
so she carried on.

After a while, her dad came in. "I've just had a phone call from the Bakers," he said. "They're going to come round later to see Nibbles."

Mr Hope looked in the cage. "He's looking a bit better," he said.

Mandy looked closely. Nibbles still wasn't moving. But his eyes did look brighter, and he had stopped trembling. "I've been stroking him," she told her dad.

"Well, carry on," Mr Hope said, smiling. "Nibbles seems to be liking it." Then he went to start Animal Ark's Saturday morning surgery.

Mandy kept stroking Nibbles and talking softly to him.

Soon, the door to the residential unit opened. Her dad came in with Laura and Mr Baker. A tearstained Tom was with them too. The little boy was clutching a bag of apple pieces.

"Nibbles!" Laura cried, running over to the cage.

At the sound of Laura's voice, Mandy saw Nibbles's ears twitch. He raised his head a little, and saw his owner. His nose wobbled once. Then he made a huge effort, and hopped bravely to the front of the cage.

"Well!" said Mr Hope, looking very surprised. "That's a good sign!"

"Oh, Nibbles," Laura whispered.

The little rabbit nudged his black nose against the wire of the cage.

Laura tickled his face with her finger. "Does this mean he's going to get better, Mr Hope?" she asked.

"It certainly looks like it," Mandy's dad replied. "He must be a very brave bunny, Laura. I didn't expect him to make such a quick recovery!" He opened the cage door and gently handed Nibbles to his owner.

Mandy felt so happy as she looked at Laura cuddling Nibbles. Everyone was smiling.

"Can I take him home now?" Laura asked.

"I think it might be best if he stays here for one more night," said Mr Hope. "Just to make sure he's completely recovered."

Laura looked disappointed but she nodded.

Tom pulled on Mr Baker's hand. "Can I give Nibbles a bit of apple, Uncle Peter?" he whispered shyly.

Mr Baker looked at Mr Hope. "Would that be all right?"

"His tummy may still be

feeling sore," Mr Hope said to the little boy. "He might not want it. But you can try."

Mr Baker lifted up up to Nibbles's cage. "I'm sorry you've been poorly, Nibbles," he said quietly.

The rabbit's nose twitched. Slowly, he reached out and took the piece of apple from Tom.

Mr Hope grinned. "Yes, he's certainly feeling better!"

*

The next day, Mr Baker, Laura and Tom came round to take Nibbles home. Mandy went with them. Laura carried Nibbles in his cardboard box.

"I've pulled up all the buttercups," Mr Baker said, as they walked down the garden. He looked down at Tom. "And I've mended the hole in the fence, so that even if Nibbles does get out, he should be safe," he added.

"But I won't *ever* let Nibbles out again without asking you, Laura," Tom said seriously.

"I know, Tom," said Laura, smiling at her cousin.

She looked up at her dad. "Can I let Nibbles have a quick run round the garden now, please?" she begged. "I know it would cheer him up!"

Mr Baker laughed. "Well, I suppose that will be all right," he said. "He can't get into much trouble now."

Laura put down the box and lifted Nibbles out onto the grass.

The little rabbit looked round for a bit. He twitched his nose and flicked his ears. Then he began to hop across the lawn.

Everyone smiled as they saw the little rabbit frisk away.

But suddenly Mr Baker didn't look quite so pleased. "He's heading for my lettuces!" he cried.

Nibbles had reached the vegetable patch. He looked cheekily at Mr Baker and then took a great big nibble out of the nearest lettuce.

Laura ran after Nibbles and scooped him up.

Mandy laughed. "It looks like Nibbles really *is* better now!" she said.

Chapter One

"Hello, Duchess!" called Mandy Hope as she walked home from school with her dad.

The white Persian cat was sunning herself on the lawn. She slowly opened her blue eyes and had a stretch. Then she wandered over to say hello.

"I see Duchess is helping you again, Jane!" Mr Hope called to Duchess's owner, Jane Parry.

Jane was a gardener. In all the gardens she worked in, Duchess was there, keeping her company.

Jane looked up from the flowerbed she was weeding at the other end of the garden. She laughed, and waved hello. "Yes," she agreed. "But Duchess doesn't ever tire herself out or get her paws dirty. She just likes to watch – or snooze!"

Mandy ran her fingers through Duchess's long fluffy coat. The cat began to purr, and rubbed her soft face against Mandy's hand.

"She'd let you stroke her like that all day, Mandy," Jane said, smiling.

Mandy smiled back. "I wouldn't mind!" she said. "Duchess is one of the nicest cats I know."

Suddenly Jane looked a bit sad. "You're right, Mandy," she said. "Duchess is a very special cat. I'm really going to miss her." She took off her gardening gloves and came over to give her pet a cuddle.